STORM

A SWEET ROMANCE NOVELLA

T. Thomas

For Riley, my reason for everything that I do.

I love you.

OTHER BOOKS BY T. THOMAS

https://thomastbooks.webador.com

T. THOMAS

©December 2021. T. Thomas. All rights reserved.

No part of this book may be reproduced, distributed, or transmitted in any form or by any means, including photocopying, recording, or other electronic or mechanical systems, without written permission from the author, except for the use of brief quotations in a book review.

This book is a work of fiction. Names, characters, places, and incidents are either a product of the author's imagination or are used fictitiously, and any resemblance to actual persons, living or dead, events, or locales is entirely coincidental.

Cover design: Tiff Writes Romance

Editing: Tiff Writes Romance

Proofreading: Taylor Jade, Kimberly Peterson

ONE

I wrapped the tape around my hands while I eyed the man in the other corner of the ring. He was older – probably somewhere in his thirties, and he was grinning, laughing at me.

He thought this would be an easy match.

The joke was on him.

I was an incredible fighter, and my small frame made me more agile than his larger body would make him. He would have a hard time keeping up with me. Being small had its advantages.

"You paired me with a scrawny little girl?" he asked his trainer. Both of them laughed.

"Don't let his words get to you," Kyle coached me. I just grunted. "You've got this in the bag. You're an incredible fighter – remember that – and don't lose sight of it. Focus on blocking your weak spot and get this fight over with," he instructed me.

Kyle had been my oldest brother's trainer. My oldest brother had been brutally murdered, and I wanted revenge. The cops had done *nothing* to find his murderer.

So, when I found out exactly *how* my brother had been murdered, I had come to Kyle, begging him to train me.

He had been reluctant at first, but he had quickly gotten on board with it when he finally figured out that I was *not* going to take no for an answer.

I wanted revenge, and I *vowed* to have it.

Nodding at Kyle to let him know I understood what he said, I let him slip my mouth guard in my mouth. The referee blew his whistle, and the guy across the ring moved towards me, swinging his fist at a rapid speed. I quickly ducked, sending a punishing blow to his ribs that I knew he wasn't expecting from someone as little as me. He stumbled back in shock at the force of my punch, and I used that to my advantage, raining blows on his face one after the other until he was sprawled out beneath me, knocked out cold.

These days, fighting guys his size was like taking candy from a baby.

The ref grabbed my arm and threw it up in the air, the man's blood trickling down my arm from my hand as he announced me as the winner of the fight by knockout. "And my beautiful ladies and incredible men, there you have it! Let's hear it for Storm!" the announcer roared.

The crowd's cheers were almost deafening, but I didn't grin or smile. I just waited for the referee to drop my arm, and once he did, I slid out of the ring and met Kyle on the side.

I didn't do this for the fame or for the money.

I had only one goal in mind, and once that was taken care of, I would quit this.

Kyle instantly led me back to his office. He grimaced at the look of my hands once he shut the door behind us.

"Doesn't ever matter how much tape you use, your hands still manage to get banged up," he admitted, watching as I unwrapped the tape from my hands.

I shrugged, tossing the bloody tape into the garbage can, moving over to his small bathroom where I washed my hands, revealing the cuts on my knuckles and fingers from busting up that cocky guy's face.

One day, these men and women would learn that I wasn't the girl they wanted to screw with.

"There's a new guy fighting tonight." I looked over at Kyle, arching my eyebrow. "Story is that he just moved here from the west coast. I looked him up – the guy was a phenomenal fighter back at his old ring. Want to check out how decent this guy is?" Kyle asked me as I stepped back out of the bathroom.

"Sure; why not?" I asked, snatching my plain black t-shirt from my duffel bag before I followed him out of the office.

I shrugged the shirt on, allowing Kyle's much larger body to lead me through the crowd until we were near the ring. I could hear the murmurs, the questions everyone had about the new guy.

They were much like the questions I had first heard when I had started fighting about two years ago, but now, I was a crowd favorite. Everyone loved me, and my name was normally a feared, yet highly respected one.

The referee slid between the ropes into the ring. "Alright, my favorite ladies and my sexy gents, first up from Phoenix, Arizona, we have Travis White, weighing in at two hundred and fifty-seven pounds! Let's hear it for the man!" the ref shouted, making the crowd go wild. I silently watched the exchange of bets before I dragged my eyes back to the stage where a beefier man was standing, and my lips twitched slightly.

He had been one of my first fights – outside of the ring, that is. I'd gotten my butt royally kicked, and I hadn't seen him around much since. He sent me a single nod, though – a nod of respect. I simply let a small smirk tilt my lips as I inclined my head towards him.

"And next up, brand new here from Los Angeles, California, we have Cayne Reynolds, weighing in at one hundred and ninety-five pounds! Let's hear it for the man!"

There weren't as many cheers for him as there were for Travis, and I knew why. The crowd didn't know him. He was new here, and it was going to take him a minute to get a fan base. And judging by the look on Travis's face, he wasn't going to end up gaining a fan base anytime tonight.

Cayne stepped into the ring, a pair of athletic shorts riding low on his hips, his hands completely bare, with no tape or anything else to protect his hands. His arms were thick, the bulging muscles flexing with every move that he made. His chest was wide and hard, and below that were even more delicious abs that drew not only my eyes but the eyes of many other girls and women in the arena. His hair was dark and messy, and his stunning, blue eyes took in everything around him so easily, yet I had a feeling those eyes didn't miss a thing.

"You two know the rules," the ref stated before he slid off of the stage.

"You think you can just show up here expecting to fight anyone you want?" Travis snapped at Cayne, a sick grin on his lips. Cayne just stared back at him coldly, his eyes emotionless as he waited for Travis to make a move, his form completely relaxed.

"Your mother seemed to think I could last night," Cayne spoke smoothly, his tone coming off bored.

My mouth dropped open in astonishment. That was a bold line.

Travis's face reddened with rage, and he swung his fist out. Cayne quickly blocked it, and swung his other fist, clocking Travis so hard across the face that he spun to the floor, blood spilling from his mouth onto the white mat.

"This is boring," I saw Cayne mutter before he slung Travis over so the man was on his back and rained two more punishing blows, knocking Travis out clean beneath him.

The crowd went wild. Travis was one of the best fighters I'd ever known, and if this newbie was able to defeat him, that meant something.

Cayne Reynolds was an excellent fighter – a heck of a lot better than me, that was for sure.

His eyes met mine as the ref lifted his arm up in the air. A slight smirk tilted his lips. Curling my lip in disgust at him and rolling my eyes, I turned on my heel and walked away, pushing through the crowd to get back to Kyle's office.

"The kid is fantastic," Kyle admitted as we stepped into his office.

"One fight doesn't show anything," I reminded Kyle.

Kyle shrugged. "He just knocked out Travis with three hits, Storm. You've got to admit that you're a bit impressed as well."

I was, but I wasn't going to admit that out loud.

Instead, I carelessly shrugged and grabbed my duffel off the floor. "I'll be back here after school tomorrow for some more practice," I informed him.

Kyle nodded. "I'll be here, Storm." He always was.

I pulled my house keys out of the side of my duffel and stuffed them into my pocket before I strode out of the old warehouse-turned-gym.

It was time to head home to hell.

~ * ~ * ~

Dressed in a pair of dark-wash skinny jeans and a plain, gray t-shirt covered by my leather jacket, I let my black combat boots pound the concrete steps as I marched up the stairs to the entrance of the building I needed on campus. I stepped in, instantly annoyed by the amount of noise surrounding me.

How did these people manage to like each other so much to the point that they had this much to talk about? I would never understand it.

I liked silence and solitude. College was just another form of torture.

My eyes fell on a familiar figure, and I had to cover my shock at seeing him there.

from me. "Let's go burn this thing," he told me. "You'll never have to look at it again," he promised.

Grabbing my hand in his, he led me over to the burn pit and tossed the dress in before turning me around in his arms and holding me tightly. "I love you," Cayne whispered, his words meant only for my ears. I squeezed my eyes shut, my heart swelling in my chest. I trembled in his arms. "I didn't realize it until you were taken from me and I was left wondering if you were going to be alive the next time that I saw you." He swallowed thickly, his Adams apple bobbing in his throat. "I want to call you mine, Storm. I want you to be my girlfriend." He looked down at me. "From the very first day that I met you, you've intrigued me. The way you fought, the way you faced the world with your chin tilted up and that defiant gleam in your eyes – I've wanted you from that very moment." He reached up and cupped my cheek. "I want you to be mine, Storm. Is that okay?"

I nodded, my eyes awash with tears. "Yes, that's okay," I croaked. I reached up and trailed my fingers over his stubble-covered jaw. He looked so tired and worn out – as if he'd had the weight of the world on his shoulders while I was missing. "I love you, too," I whispered. "I want nothing more than for you to finally call me yours."

He leaned down and took my lips in a sweet kiss, and somehow, I knew that was all he wanted from me - all he would ever expect from me.

I'd just gone through hell and back, lived with the fear that I may forever be tied to a monster.

But I was happy here with Cayne, and somehow, I knew this was exactly where I was meant to be.

EPILOGUE

College was officially freaking over.

We had finally graduated and were on to the next chapter of our lives: being working adults.

Camron had majored in physical education and was taking a teaching job that started in the fall at the local elementary school.

Cayne had majored in business management, and he had gotten hired on at the last place he did his internship with. It was a job that paid extremely well and allowed him to take Kellian to school and be off in time to pick him up. He worked directly under the CEO since he had major analytical skills, and the CEO was surprisingly extremely understandable about Cayne being Kellian's father figure.

I had majored in psychology and was taking a job as a secretary at a local therapist's office while I got my master's in trauma therapy.

I had to go through a crap ton of therapy to move past what had happened to me. I woke up every night for *months* with nightmares of marrying Elijah and flashbacks of killing him. Though I had done it as an act of self-defense – at least that's what the judge ruled it as – it still didn't settle right with me that I had killed someone.

That wasn't the only thing that I had to go to therapy for though.

I also had to go to therapy to move past Miguel's brutal murder and to also get help with my abandonment issues from all of the crap surrounding my parents.

Camron suddenly wrapped his arms around me and spun me around in a circle. I squealed. "Camron, put me down!" I yelled, smacking my older brother. "You're making me dizzy!"

He laughed and set me on my feet, pressing a kiss to the top of my head. "We did it, Sis. We freaking graduated."

I beamed at him. It hadn't been easy juggling regular jobs and going to school, especially since I also lived with Cayne and helped raise Kellian, but Camron was right.

We had done it.

Cayne popped up near me with Kellian on his shoulders. Kellian high-fived me, yelling *congratulations* at the top of his lungs. I laughed and beamed at him. Kellian was such a sweetheart.

"Ready to head back to our place?" Cayne asked me, grabbing my hand in his and bringing it up to his lips to press a kiss to the back of my hand.

"Yeah," I told him. "I'm starving." I looked at Camron. "Will you be over?"

Camron nodded at me. "I'll be there as soon as I get home and change out of these clothes," he told me. "I'll pick up some pizzas on my way."

"Thanks," Cayne told him, speaking over his brother yelling his excitement about pizza. Camron gave me a hug before walking off, heading towards the car park.

That was another thing about Camron. He never left my presence without at least hugging me. When I went missing, it screwed with him badly, too. He was always terrified that something would happen to rip me from his life again.

Cayne wrapped an arm around my shoulders, and together, we walked to the car park, neither of us having families there to congratulate us like everyone else did.

But that worked for us because Cayne, Camron, and Kellian were all the family that I needed.

~ * ~ * ~

I slipped into bed beside Cayne, giggling when he wrapped his arms around me from behind, nuzzling his nose against the back of my neck.

"I was wondering when you were going to bring your cute behind to bed," he teased.

I laughed. "I had to brush my hair and my teeth," I told him. It was my nightly routine. After almost three years together, he should know my routine.

He scoffed and reached behind him, grabbing something before wrapping his arm back around me. He flipped open a black, velvet box. A gasp left my lips as I stared at the simple, diamond ring in front of me.

"Storm, I love you." Tears burned in my eyes. "You mean the world to me. I would give anything to see your smile every single day of my life. You accepted me despite me being a dad to my little brother, and I love that you still face the world with your chin held high despite everything you've gone through."

A tear slipped down my cheek.

I couldn't believe that this was happening.

"Marry me," he whispered. He pressed a kiss to my shoulder. "Please marry me, Storm. I want you to be my wife."

I rolled over to face him, trying not to cry, but another tear betrayed me and slipped free, rolling down on my cheek. "On one condition," I croaked.

He grinned at me. "Name it."

I laughed. He was never one to back down. "We have to get married in Vegas. No wedding dress." A chill raced down my spine. His eyes softened with understanding. "No tuxes. I just want to get married by Elvis in the trashiest wedding possible."

He leaned forward, taking my lips in a soft kiss. "Understandable." I relaxed. "Deal, babe. Looks like we need to start looking at tickets for Vegas."

I giggled as he grabbed my hand and slipped my ring on my finger before wrapping me up in his arms, his lips meeting mine again. "Thank you," he murmured against my lips.

"For?" I asked him, opening my eyes to look deep into his blue ones, easily losing myself in them.

He brushed his nose with mine in an Eskimo kiss. "For making me the happiest man alive tonight," he told me. "I love you, Storm."

I beamed at him, cupping his cheek with the hand that now held my engagement ring, loving the way it glittered in the moonlight. "And I love you," I whispered. I swallowed thickly. "Thank you for saving me, Cayne, in more ways than one."

He covered my hand with his, turning his head to press a kiss to my palm before focusing those startling, blue eyes back on my face. "Always, baby."

WANT MORE BOOKS BY T. THOMAS?

https://thomastbooks.webador.com

STORM

PLEASE LEAVE A REVIEW!

I would love to see your thoughts!

If possible, please leave a review on Amazon:

https://books2read.com/stormtthomas

FOLLOW T. THOMAS

Facebook: https://www.facebook.com/authorthomast

Facebook group:
https://www.facebook.com/groups/thomast

Instagram:
https://www.instagram.com/authorthomast

ABOUT THE AUTHOR

T. Thomas is a sweet romance author.

She has been writing since she was thirteen years old. She enjoys spending all of her spare time writing, but she absolutely detests editing and proofreading.

T. Thomas can normally be found in her little room of her own that she calls her "woman cave" writing her next book and putting off editing and proofreading for as long as possible.